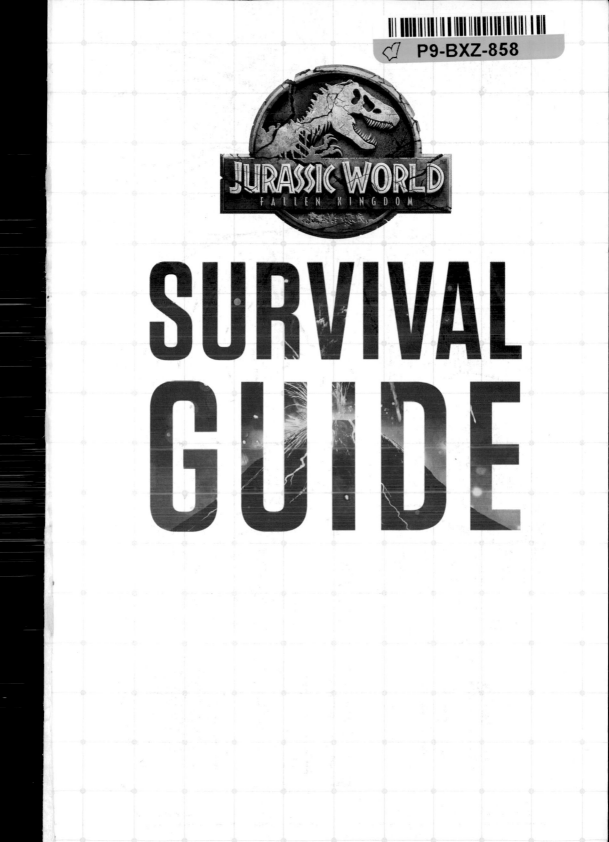

JURASSIC WORLD™
FALLEN KINGDOM

SURVIVAL GUIDE

rhcbooks.com

ISBN 978-0-525-58083-6 (tr. pbk.) – ISBN 978-0-525-58084-3 (lib. bdg.) –
ISBN 978-0-525-58085-0 (ebook)

10 9 8 7 6 5 4 3

Printed in the United States of America

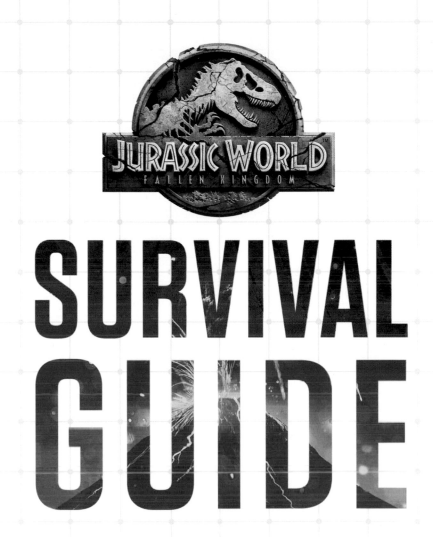

SURVIVAL GUIDE

by David Lewman

Random House 🏠 New York

CONTENTS

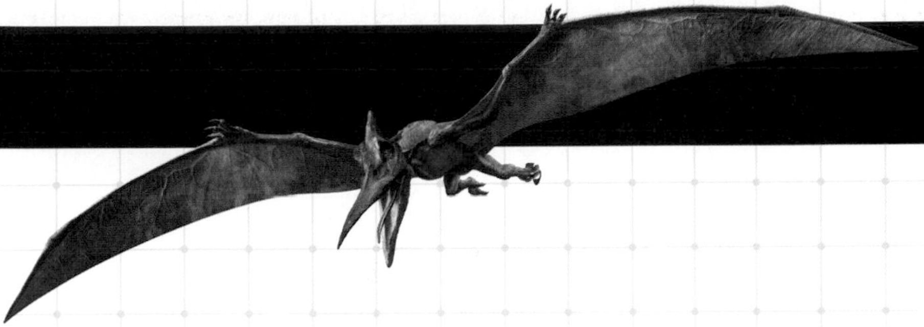

CONFIDENTIAL
MEMO

FROM: Claire Dearing, Dinosaur
      Protection Group

TO: Newest Team Members

CLASSIFICATION: TOP-SECRET

Team Members:

   Our mission is to rescue the dinosaurs on Isla Nublar before the volcano erupts. This task is tremendously important, but it is also *extremely dangerous.* Since we don't know when the volcano will erupt, we'll have to move quickly. If I seem a bit abrupt or curt, that's because time is of the essence.

   To help ensure your survival, please study these materials carefully. This is all *highly classified* information. In the future, these documents may prove valuable to others who care about the fate of these magnificent creatures. But for now, share these contents with absolutely *no one.*

I've put this packet together quickly, since the mission was organized at the last second. I've gathered as much information as I could about the place we're going and the dangers we may face there. Other team members have contributed valuable insights, as you'll see.

There should be plenty of time on our flight to read this dossier. I *strongly* suggest you thoroughly familiarize yourself with the contents.

Thank you for undertaking this dangerous but vital mission. *Let's all be safe out there!*

Owen,

I realize you know more about surviving dinosaur encounters than any of us, but I still think you should take a look at this guide.

Thanks,
Claire

WHERE WE'RE GOING

This a map of Isla Nublar, the site of the former theme park Jurassic World. As you can see, the volcano is at the north end of the island. Since it could erupt at any time, we'll be staying as far away from it as possible!

The group we are joining plans to head down Main Street and through Gyrosphere Valley to a bunker underneath a radio tower. Once there, I'll use my handprint to access the park's dinosaur tracking system, making it easier for us to locate and rescue the remaining dinosaurs.

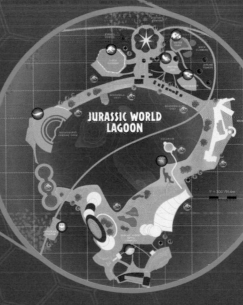

In the years since the unfortunate events at the park, much will have changed. Dinosaurs have roamed the island unchecked. Vegetation has grown wild. Storms have taken their toll. So when it comes to the accuracy of this map, all bets are off. Use it as a general guide at best.

JURASSIC WORLD LAGOON

MISSION BACKGROUND

Please review the time line below and commit it to memory. It includes some of the milestones that have led to our current mission. Not only is the information fascinating, it might prove vital during our time on Isla Nublar.

1984: Dr. John Parker Hammond and his company, InGen, successfully cloned the first prehistoric animal from DNA preserved in amber. His silent partner in this venture was philanthropist Benjamin Lockwood.

1986: The first dinosaur—a *Triceratops*—was successfully cloned by InGen at Isla Sorna, off the coast of Costa Rica. Initially, it was difficult to know what type of dinosaur was going to be created from the DNA trapped in the amber, but subsequent successes—especially those of Dr. Henry Wu—quickly refined the process.

1988: John Hammond promoted Dr. Wu to chief geneticist and started building Jurassic Park on Isla Nublar, also off the coast of Costa Rica. Later that same year, mature cloned animals were moved from Isla Sorna, where they were created, to Jurassic Park on Isla Nublar. They were housed in temporary paddocks until permanent park structures were completed.

1992: Jurassic Park game warden Robert Muldoon discovered that *Velociraptors* were displaying high levels of shared intelligence, solving tasks through cooperation and coordinating their attacks.

1993: John Hammond took his grandchildren and a team of experts (including Dr. Ian Malcolm, an authority on chaos theory; paleobotanist Dr. Ellie Sattler; and paleontologist Dr. Alan Grant) to Isla Nublar for a pre-opening tour of Jurassic Park.

It did not go well.

A TROPICAL STORM HIT THE ISLAND DURING THE TOUR, AND THE DINOSAURS WERE ABLE TO BREACH THE ELECTRIC FENCES. AS A RESULT, THE T. REX AND SEVERAL VELOCIRAPTORS ESCAPED. SADLY, SEVERAL HUMAN LIVES WERE LOST, AND THE PLANS TO OPEN THE PARK WERE IMMEDIATELY CANCELED. INVESTIGATORS SUSPECTED THAT ONE OR MORE JURASSIC PARK EMPLOYEES WERE RESPONSIBLE IN SOME WAY FOR THIS TRAGIC EVENT, BUT WE MAY NEVER KNOW THE TRUTH.

LIVES LOST

Lawyer
Donald Gennaro:
Devoured by *T. rex*

Game warden
Robert Muldoon:
Killed by *Velociraptors*

Computer programmer
Dennis Nedry:
Killed by *Dilophosaurus*

Chief Engineer
Ray Arnold:
Killed by *Velociraptors*

1994: Dr. Wu returned to Jurassic Park on Isla Nublar to assist in the cleanup and in the cataloging of dinosaurs.

1997: Under the leadership of Hammond's nephew, Peter Ludlow, InGen raided Isla Sorna to acquire dinosaurs for the once-planned Jurassic Park: San Diego.

LIVES LOST

Engineer
Eddie Carr:
Devoured by *T. rex*

Dinosaur expert
Dr. Robert Burke:
Devoured by *T. rex*

InGen hunter
Dieter Stark:
Killed by *Compsognathus*

THIS MISSION PROVED UNSUCCESSFUL. SOMEHOW, SEVERAL CAGED
DINOSAURS WERE RELEASED WITHIN THE CONFINES OF THE INGEN
CAMP. UNFORTUNATELY, THERE WERE NUMEROUS CASUALTIES, AND
THE CAMP WAS COMPLETELY DESTROYED.

THE SURVIVING MEMBERS OF THE INGEN TEAM WERE ABLE TO
SUCCESSFULLY TRANSPORT AN ADULT T. REX TO SAN DIEGO. THE
T. REX ESCAPED AND WAS RECAPTURED, BUT NOT BEFORE CAUSING
CONSIDERABLE DAMAGE TO THE SURROUNDING AREAS. SHE WAS
FINALLY RETURNED TO ISLA SORNA, AND PLANS FOR JURASSIC PARK:
SAN DIEGO WERE ABANDONED.

1997: Simon Masrani, CEO of the Masrani Corporation, an international company with interests in oil, telecom, mining, construction, health care, and most importantly, genetics, met with John Hammond and began talks to acquire InGen. John Hammond died later that year.

1998: Masrani Global Corporation acquired InGen. Simon Masrani began planning a new theme park on Isla Nublar—Jurassic World— with the help of Dr. Wu.

2001: In an attempt to save their missing son, Paul and Amanda Kirby hired a group of armed mercenaries to search Isla Sorna. Their search party included Dr. Alan Grant, as well as his assistant, Billy Brennan.

Though the Kirbys succeeded in rescuing their son, the mission was disastrous. There were several fatalities, and the group accidentally let *Pteranodons* escape from their aviary.

The survivors had to be rescued by members of the United States Armed Forces.

Later that year, the *Pteranodons* were captured over Canada by a cleanup team led by Vic Hoskins. Masrani later hired Hoskins as a security expert at Jurassic World.

What Masrani didn't know was that Hoskins was also secretly interested in developing a program to turn dinosaurs into weapons of war.

LIVES LOST

Mercenary
Cooper:
Devoured by *Spinosaurus*

Pilot
M. B. Nash:
Devoured by *Spinosaurus*

Mercenary
Udesky:
Killed by *Velociraptors*

2002–2004: Masrani Corporation built Jurassic World on Isla Nublar.

2004: Dinosaurs were moved from Isla Sorna to Isla Nublar.

2012: As the novelty of the park wore off, attendance slipped. Therefore, Masrani and I authorized Dr. Wu to create a new hybrid. That same year, Hoskins hired naval officer Owen Grady for InGen's Integrated Behavioral Raptor Intelligence Study (IBRIS).

2005: On May 30, Jurassic World opened to the public. The park was an instant success. In the first year alone, over eight million visitors from more than ninety countries attended. For the first ten years, operations were *relatively* smooth.

2015: Before being put on display, the new hybrid dinosaur, Indominus Rex, escaped from its enclosure.

Once free, the Indominus Rex broke a hole in the *Pteranodon* aviary. Escaped *Pteranodons* smashed into a helicopter piloted by Simon Masrani. He died in the crash.

He was a good man and didn't deserve to go that way.

2015: Dr. Henry Wu fled the island. Many believe he took genetic material with him to continue his research elsewhere.

Let's hope not—for all our sakes.

Vic Hoskins intended to use *Velociraptors* as military weapons but was killed by one instead.

The Indominus Rex was killed by the *Mosasaurus*.

Jurassic World was closed and abandoned. Dinosaurs of several species have since roamed free on Isla Nublar.

LIVES LOST

Industrialist
Simon Masrani:
Killed in helicopter crash caused by *Pteranodons*

Executive assistant
Zara Shealy:
Devoured by *Pteranodons* and *Mosasaurus*

Security expert
Vic Hoskins:
Killed by *Velociraptor*

19

Since the Closing of Jurassic World

Dr. Henry Wu was found guilty of bioethical misconduct and stripped of all his credentials.

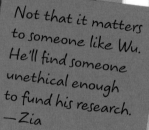

Not that it matters to someone like Wu. He'll find someone unethical enough to fund his research.
—Zia

Isla Nublar's long-dormant volcano has become active, threatening to erupt and kill all the dinosaurs on the island.

The Masrani Corporation denied any responsibility for the survival of the dinosaurs on Isla Nublar.

DINOSAUR PROTECTION GROUP

The Dinosaur Protection Group was founded to save these living creatures.

Philanthropist Benjamin Lockwood revealed himself as the longtime silent partner of John Hammond.

Lockwood is funding our rescue mission to Isla Nublar. His assistant, Eli Mills, is arranging for all the transport vehicles and personnel necessary for the dinosaurs to be safely taken to the sanctuary Lockwood has built for them.

For these purposes, the following team has been assembled: Owen Grady, Zia Rodriguez, Franklin Webb, and me, Claire Dearing.

OWEN GRADY

I'll introduce you to some other players later on, but let me get you acquainted with the rest of your team before we go any further. We'll be your family out there on the island. Your life is in our hands, and ours are in yours.

Owen Grady is the team's animal behaviorist. We look to Owen for expertise on how to safely capture dinosaurs for transport to Benjamin Lockwood's island sanctuary. He is especially knowledgeable about Blue, the *Velociraptor* who imprinted on Owen when she was just a hatchling. They have a special relationship unprecedented in human-dinosaur history.

Grady is a former naval officer. During his time in the navy, he worked on many covert animal training programs, including ████, ██████, and giant ██████, as well as ██████, ████, and genetically modified ██████████ with razor-sharp teeth.

Sorry, Claire.
It's classified.
—Owen

In 2012, Vic Hoskins hired Grady to work on InGen Security's Integrated Behavioral Raptor Intelligence Study. For three years, Owen worked with *Velociraptors* on Isla Nublar, seeing whether they could be trained and socialized.

In 2013, Owen warned Hoskins about the complexities of *Velociraptor* pack dynamics. Two years later, Hoskins was killed by a *Velociraptor*.

In 2015, Owen was instrumental in stopping the Indominus Rex and saving Jurassic World personnel (including me).

If you have any questions about how to survive on Isla Nublar, Owen is the first person to ask. But don't tell him I told you so. It'll go straight to his head.

I did warn him —Owen

DEFEND
ISLA
NUBLAR
OCCUPANTS
DINO

ON THE PLANET!
1ST
ON THE PLANET!

CLAIRE DEARING

Claire Dearing rose through the ranks at Masrani Corporation, where she started as an intern and grew to become the operations manager of Jurassic World. Her specialty was bringing corporate sponsorship to the park. But don't let the stiff corporate background fool you. I'm sure you've heard about her heroics saving her nephews at Jurassic World. She was all over the news for months.

Claire doesn't know I'm adding her bio in here, so I hope you can keep it a secret. — Zia

Following the disaster at the park in 2015, she took some time off to decide what her next move would be.

Claire was disillusioned by the corporate world and no longer interested in working for a group driven solely by profit. She founded the Dinosaur Protection Group, a not-for-profit organization dedicated to saving the animals left stranded on Isla Nublar. When the island's volcano threatened to erupt, the group's mission became urgent.

A couple of days ago, she agreed to join a mission to Isla Nublar and help rescue the dinosaurs for transportation to a secret sanctuary that this rich guy, Mr. Lockwood, has set up to keep the dinosaurs far from the threats of volcanoes and mankind.

Claire's years working at Jurassic World have given her invaluable knowledge of Isla Nublar. Probably most important, she's a survivor who is as dedicated to her team's safety as she is to her own.

EVACUATE ISLA NUBLAR NOW!

DINOSAUR PROTECTION GROUP

A SURVIVAL TIP: When all else fails —RUN! —Claire

PERSONNEL FILES

ZIA RODRIGUEZ

Zia Rodriguez is the team's paleoveterinarian, a specialist in providing medical care for dinosaurs. And before you ask if that's a real job, it is. And she's darned good at it.

Her participation in this mission is crucial, since we don't know what kind of health challenges the dinosaurs might be facing after three years of unassisted life on Isla Nublar.

She will supervise the sedation of dangerous dinosaurs for safe transport.

Should any medical emergencies arise during our mission, Zia will lead the response. Please assist her in any way she asks.

If her manner ever seems slightly impatient, it's only because Zia is deeply passionate about saving these beautiful creatures and recognizes the urgency and importance of our mission.

> Thanks,
> Claire!
> — Zia

> Owen,
> please note!
> —Claire

DINOSAUR
PROTECTION
GROUP

WE CAN SAVE THEM

#WECANSAVETHEM

A SURVIVAL TIP: *Trust yourself. Your own mind can be your worst enemy!* —Zia

FRANKLIN WEBB

Franklin Webb is the team's systems architect. (He doesn't like to be called a "computer guy," so please refrain from referring to Franklin as such.)

He's a graduate of the prestigious Massachusetts Institute of Technology and is highly skilled when it comes to building and maintaining complex computer architecture—and when necessary, hacking secure computer systems.

Hired by the Dinosaur Protection Group, he became our social media coordinator.

Should we encounter any technological hurdles on this mission, Franklin's our man.

SERIOUSLY. I AM SO MUCH MORE THAN A SOCIAL MEDIA COORDINATOR.
—FRANKLIN

ALL ENDANGERED SPECIES ARE EQUAL

SAVE THE DINOS!

DINOSAUR PROTECTION GROUP

A SURVIVAL TIP: Never volunteer for a mission like this. —Franklin

DINOSAURS
WE MAY ENCOUNTER

BRACHIOSAURUS
21.5 M LONG X 12.4 M TALL

T. REX
13.5 M LONG X 5.2 M TALL

APATOSAURUS
27.4 M LONG X 6.1 M TALL

TRICERATOPS
8.9 M LONG X 3.6 M TALL

STEGOSAU
10.1 M LONG X

MOSASAURUS
21.9 M LONG

DINO SIZE CHART

ACHYRHINOSAURUS
.1 M LONG X 4.2 M TALL

PTERANODON
7.5 M WINGSPAN
X 3.1 M LONG

CARNOTAURUS
10.4 M LONG X 2.9 M TALL

GALLIMIMUS
4.7 M LONG X 3.0 M TALL

INDORAPTOR
7.3 M LONG X 3.1 M TALL

BLUE (RAPTOR)
3.9 M LONG X 1.7 M TALL

STYGIMOLOCH
3.5 M LONG X 1.4 M TALL

ANKYLOSAURUS
9.6 M LONG X 3.6 M TALL

COMPIES (COMPSOGNATHUS)
0.77 M LONG X 0.6 M TALL

BARYONYX
9.3 M LONG X 2.65 M TALL

ALLOSAURUS
12.1 M LONG X 3.8 M TALL

VELOCIRAPTOR
BLUE

BLOOD SAMPLES

SAMPLE 01 | SAMPLE 02 | SAMPLE 03 | SAMPLE 04 | SAMPLE 05 | SAMPLE 06 | SAMPLE 07

Assuming she's still alive, Blue is the sole surviving *Velociraptor*, trained from birth by Owen. From infancy, Blue has shown remarkable intelligence and empathy (at least toward Owen).

No idea of her long-term memory. I could be a stranger to her now.

But she's not a trained pet. Blue is still a deadly predator. She's smart, fast, and potentially vicious, with extremely sharp claws and teeth.

The few people who have studied live Velociraptors have suggested that they may be the second-most intelligent species on the planet after humans.

—Owen

SPECIES: *Velociraptor*

NAME MEANING: "Swift thief"

LENGTH: 11 feet, 10 inches

DISTINCTIVE MARKS: Long blue stripes running along both sides of spine, one of which stretches from eye to tip of tail.

DANGEROUS FEATURES: Long, strong arms. Razor-sharp, retractable sickle claws. Sharp, deadly teeth. Powerful tail.

SKILLS: Can smell prey a mile off. Able to cooperate socially and hunt in packs. Great speed and leaping ability.

X-RAY // 00000001

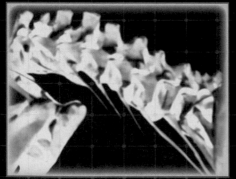

X-RAY // 00000002

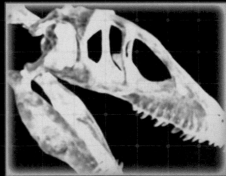

OWEN'S DOS and DON'TS

DO stick to open spaces—no grassy fields.

DON'T turn your back on Blue.

DO stay behind me—I'm the Alpha.

DON'T try to outthink Blue.

DO distract her (if you can) with beef jerky and dead rats.

DON'T try to use hand signals you haven't trained with before.

Leave it to me!
I'm a professional.
OWEN

MOSASAURUS

The *Mosasaurus* is not a dinosaur. She's a carnivorous marine lizard.

Recent sightings suggest that the *Mosasaurus* has escaped from her Jurassic World enclosure and hunts for food in the open waters surrounding Isla Nublar.

The *Mosasaurus* was by far the largest animal ever exhibited at Jurassic World.

Just because you're not in the water doesn't mean you're safe from a *Mosasaurus*, which has been known to leap out onto dry land to engulf prey, just like alligators at a watering hole.

THEY BELONG HERE NOW

SPECIES: *Mosasaurus*
LENGTH: 85 feet
WEIGHT: 64,000 pounds
DANGEROUS FEATURES: Double row of spikes down spine. Cavernous mouth. Double set of huge, sharp teeth. Muscular tail. Four strong fins.
SKILLS: Explosive speed in water. Great leaping ability. Tremendous jaw strength makes for crushing bite.

OWEN'S DOS AND DON'TS

DO avoid swimming anywhere near Isla Nublar.

DON'T go anywhere near the Jurassic World Lagoon.

DO keep a safe distance from the beach if possible.

DON'T shoot your tranquilizer dart at the *Mosasaurus*—you'll only make her mad!

1ST · ON THE PLANET! · ON THE PLANET!

TYRANNOSAURUS REX

The *Tyrannosaurus rex* is basically a big killing and eating machine, one of the most fearsome creatures ever to stomp its way across the planet.

There is only one *Tyrannosaurus rex* on Isla Nublar (as far as we know), but she's a force to be reckoned with, so be on your toes. Before Jurassic World was abandoned, she successfully battled the Indominus Rex, even though the Indominus had been specifically designed to be her superior. (Of course, she had a slight assist from the *Mosasaurus* and Owen's pack of Raptors.)

The *T. rex* has killed humans in the past, and as one of nature's most powerful hunters, she is likely to do so again if given the chance.

SPECIES: *Tyrannosaurus rex*

NAME MEANING: "King tyrant lizard"

LENGTH: 40 feet

WEIGHT: 18,500 pounds

DISTINCTIVE MARKS: Numerous scars from battles with *Velociraptors* and Indominus Rex.

DANGEROUS FEATURES: Thick, razor-sharp teeth capable of crushing bones. Massive jaw muscles. Powerful back legs. Two claws on each arm and three on each foot. Short but extremely strong arms.

SKILLS: Forward vision superior to that of many dinosaurs, although sight is based on movement. Keen sense of smell. Terrific speed. Overwhelming strength.

BLOOD SAMPLES

SAMPLE 01	SAMPLE 02	SAMPLE 03	SAMPLE 04	SAMPLE 05
SAMPLE 06	SAMPLE 07	SAMPLE 08	SAMPLE 09	SAMPLE 10
SAMPLE 11	SAMPLE 12	SAMPLE 13	SAMPLE 14	SAMPLE 15

TRO3ᴬ

FREE
THE
DINOSAURS

OWEN'S DOS AND DON'TS

DO feel the ground for vibrations from her footsteps.

DON'T try to outrun her.

DO distract her with a flare.

DON'T get in the way of her feet!

DO climb a **VERY** tall and **VERY** sturdy tree to escape.

STEGOSAURUS

Just because the *Stegosaurus* is a plant-eater doesn't mean she can't hurt you . . . or a *T. rex*, for that matter. This is a very tough animal, with a deadly spiked tail that she's not afraid to use.

She can move quickly. And you certainly wouldn't want to get trampled by her.

SPECIES: *Stegosaurus*

NAME MEANING: "Roofed lizard"

LENGTH: 33 feet

WEIGHT: 7,700 pounds

DISTINCTIVE FEATURES: Double row of 17 broad back plates.

DANGEROUS FEATURES: Heavy feet. Powerful spiked tail.

SKILLS: Able to swing tail with tremendous force and surprising speed.

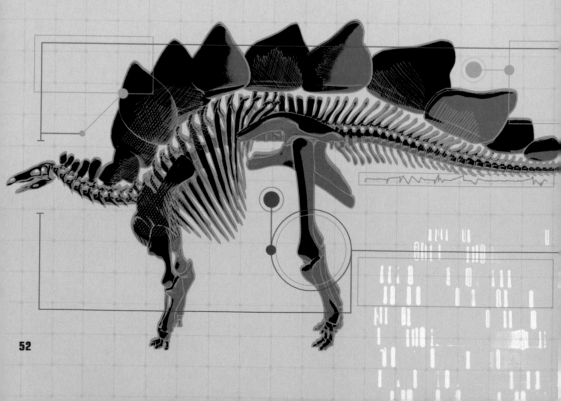

OWEN'S DOS & DON'TS

DON'T take your eyes off her tail.

DO hide if you hear her coming.

She eats plants. DON'T give her
a reason to hurt you.

DON'T assume she's slow—because
she's not!

DINOSAUR PROTECTION GROUP

PTERANODON

As flying carnivores with huge wingspans, *Pteranodons* are particularly dangerous. They've been known to attack in formation, like a squadron of fighter jets.

Pteranodons tend to roost in groups, often near cliff sides, making it easier for them to catch the wind with their wide wings.

Though toothless, *Pteranodons* have sharp, pointed beaks and strong, grasping feet that are useful for snatching prey off the ground or out of the water.

SPECIES: *Pteranodon*

NAME MEANING: "Toothless wing"

WINGSPAN: 20 feet

WEIGHT: 7 pounds

DISTINCTIVE FEATURES: Small "hands" halfway along wings. Long, pointed crest on back of head.

DANGEROUS FEATURES: Long, pointed beak. Grasping feet. Powerful wings.

SKILLS: Soaring flight. Able to swoop and dive on prey. Precision snatching with feet. Can hop across ground.

OWEN'S DOS & DON'TS

If you notice her shadow on the ground, DO take cover.

DON'T let go of her feet if in midflight. Wait until you're closer to the ground.

DO offer her fish as a distraction.

DO avoid her sharp beak, which she can use as a spear.

ANKYLOSAURUS

The *Ankylosaurus* is another herbivore that shouldn't be thought of as harmless just because she eats only plants.

    Big and heavily armored, the *Ankylosaurus* is like a walking tank. She wields her tail like a mace, swinging it right at the knees of bigger dinosaurs such as the *T. rex*.

A GOOD WAY TO REMEMBER HER NAME IS THAT THE ANKYLOSAURUS CAN MAKE YOUR ANKLES VERY SORE!
:) FRANKLIN

SPECIES: *Ankylosaurus*
NAME MEANING: "Fused lizard"
LENGTH: 32 feet
WEIGHT: 17,600 pounds
DISTINCTIVE FEATURES: Armored plates across back.
DANGEROUS FEATURES: Spikes jutting out of armor. Tail shaped like war club. Sharp beak.
SKILLS: Swinging and smashing with tail. Biting and gnashing with beak.

OWEN'S DOS & DON'TS

DO avoid her tail.

DO offer her ferns and flowering plants like magnolias as a distraction in an emergency.

DON'T mess with her and she won't mess with you.

DON'T approach when she is with her young.

And **NEVER, EVER** take your eyes off that tail!

SINOCERATOPS

This herbivore is from the same scientific family as the *Triceratops*, which will make sense when you see her large, protective frill. Fossil records indicate that this dinosaur wasn't blessed with the largest brain, so don't expect Raptor-level intelligence from this one.

SPECIES: *Sinoceratops*

NAME MEANING: "Horned face"

LENGTH: 20 feet

WEIGHT: 6,600 pounds

DISTINCTIVE FEATURES: Large frill on head with small horns protruding from the edges.

DANGEROUS FEATURES: Has been known to be a curious animal, which can unknowingly lead her close to unsuspecting humans.

SKILLS: Heightened sense of smell due to large nose.

OWEN'S DOS & DON'TS

DO remain calm. She is more afraid of you than you are of her.

DON'T wear too much cologne or perfume. She can smell you from a mile away.

DO keep still if one moves in close to smell or lick you. She will leave when she is done.

COMPSOGNATHUS

"Compies" are small meat-eaters. But don't let their size fool you—they can be deadly, especially when they attack as a group!

SPECIES: *Compsognathus*

NAME MEANING: "Delicate jaw"

LENGTH: 4 feet

WEIGHT: 2 pounds

DISTINCTIVE FEATURES: Long, slender tail. Short arms.

DANGEROUS FEATURES: Sharp teeth. Claws on hands and feet.

SKILLS: Good vision. Speed. Tearing and ripping with teeth.

OWEN'S DOS & DON'TS

DO distract them by offering her small reptiles in an emergency.

DON'T make the mistake of thinking she's "cute"!

DON'T try to outrun her.

DO stand tall to intimidate her.

DON'T let her size fool you. A swarm of Compies has taken down prey larger than humans.

With Compies, if there's one, THERE ARE MORE. —Zia

TRICERATOPS

The *Triceratops* might be the most dangerous plant-eating dinosaur of all, capable of taking on a *T. rex* in battle—and winning. She has the largest teeth of any plant-eating dinosaur. Her teeth are self-sharpening and ever-replacing. She's also fiercely protective of her young.

SAVE THE DINOS!

SPECIES: *Triceratops*

NAME MEANING: "Three-horned face"

LENGTH: 26 feet

WEIGHT: 22,000 pounds

DISTINCTIVE FEATURES: Large, solid frill on head. Long, pointed tail.

DANGEROUS FEATURES: Two long horns over eyes. One short horn over nose. Strongest jaw of any land-dwelling plant-eater ever. Large teeth.

SKILLS: Goring with horns. Ramming with head. Biting with sharp beak.

OWEN'S DOS & DON'TS

DO stay far away from her territory, especially when babies are present.

NEVER, EVER get between a mom and her baby.

DO stay on the right side of those horns.

DINOSAURS ARE PARENTS TOO!

#WECANSAVETHEM

SAVE THE DINOS

BARYONYX

Baryonyx is a fearsome meat-eating predator. Her teeth are shaped like cones instead of blades (like the teeth of other carnivorous dinosaurs). The teeth are also serrated so they can easily separate flesh from bone.

LOOKS LIKE SOMEONE
STUCK A CROCODILE'S
HEAD ON A T. REX.
—FRANKLIN

SPECIES: *Baryonyx*
NAME MEANING: "Heavy claw"
LENGTH: 30.5 feet
WEIGHT: 3,770 pounds
DISTINCTIVE FEATURES: Tail as long as body. Short arms.
DANGEROUS FEATURES: Huge pollical—or "thumb"—claw. Sharp teeth. Whiplike tail.
SKILLS: Ripping flesh with teeth. Tearing with claws. Whipping with tail.

Tail gives her good balance while fighting. —Zia

OWEN'S DOS & DON'TS

Like all dinosaurs, she's afraid of fire. So DO bring some matches.

DON'T go into the Jurassic World tunnels unless you know how to get back out in a hurry.

DON'T think you can outrun her—you can't!

STYGIMOLOCH

Stiggy won't eat you, but that doesn't mean she can't knock you across a very large room with a solid head-butt. This mostly gentle plant-eater has a thick, bony dome on top of her head. She likes to ram her tough skull into enemies, knocking them down and severely injuring them. She also has spikes on the back of her head that protect her from rear attacks and significantly increase the damage she can inflict. Luckily, her teeth are tiny.

I LIKE THE SOUND OF THIS ONE! —F.W.

SAVE THE DINOS!

SPECIES: *Stygimoloch*
NAME MEANING: "River Styx demon"
LENGTH: 7 feet
WEIGHT: 200 pounds
DISTINCTIVE FEATURES: Domed skull. Short horns over nose.
DANGEROUS FEATURES: Extra-thick skull bone. Massive spikes on back of head.
SKILLS: Butting and ramming. Goring with spikes.

OWEN'S DOS & DON'TS

DO climb to escape.

DO be on your toes and ready to dodge.

DON'T ever whistle at her—she hates that!

CARNOTAURUS

Carnotaurus is a ferocious meat-eater that is smaller but faster than *Tyrannosaurus rex*. She has two knobby horns over her eyes, giving her a devilish appearance, which is what originally drew us to cloning her for the park.

Her arms are so short, they're practically just wrists. But it's not the arms you have to watch out for: it's the teeth.

Don't forget the claws on her feet! —Zia

SPECIES: *Carnotaurus*

NAME MEANING: "Meat-eating bull"

LENGTH: 34 feet

WEIGHT: 4,800 pounds

DISTINCTIVE FEATURES:
Two thick horns. Bumpy
spines down her back.

DANGEROUS FEATURES: Long,
sharp teeth. Powerful legs.

SKILLS: Running. Butting and goring
with horns. Biting fiercely.

OWEN'S DOS & DON'TS

DO watch out for her claws.

DO try to position large objects
between you and her.

DON'T try to knock her out—her skull
is armored!

INDOMINUS REX

Part *Velociraptor*, part nightmare, the Indominus Rex is the hybrid dinosaur that brought down Jurassic World.

Though the only known specimen was killed by a *Mosasaurus*, it's not impossible that another may have hatched at some point without our knowledge. Better to be overprepared. . . .

SPECIES: Indominus Rex

NAME MEANING: "Indomitable king"

LENGTH: 50 feet

WEIGHT: 16,000 pounds

DISTINCTIVE FEATURES: White coloration. Hollows on snout in front of eyes. Spines on back of head.

DANGEROUS FEATURES: Huge mouth full of razor-sharp teeth. Long talons.

SKILLS: Senses thermal radiation. Can camouflage. Hides by changing her heat signature. Highly intelligent. Unprecedented sense of smell.

OWEN'S DOS & DON'TS

DO mask your scent with something: gasoline, even dino dung.

DON'T assume she's gone just because you don't see her.

DON'T expect *Velociraptors* to attack her.

DON'T think she'll stop when she's full—she kills for sport!

INDORAPTOR

To: Claire

From: Franklin

Preparing for this mission, I stumbled upon some of Dr. Wu's old park files. (Okay, I hacked into them. That **is** what I do. . . .) Found this. Disturbing.

Everyone—

This is very disturbing. It suggests that someone was working to cross Indominus Rex genetic material with a velociraptor. Let's hope they didn't get too far!

Claire

SPECIES: Indoraptor
NAME MEANING: "Indomitable thief"
LENGTH: 14 feet
WEIGHT: 2,200 pounds
DISTINCTIVE FEATURES: Unknown.
DANGEROUS FEATURES: Intelligence
of a *Velociraptor.* Enhanced tracking
ability. Heightened sense of smell.
Night vision.
SKILLS: Trainable. Slashing
claws. Ripping teeth.
Incredible speed.

This must be
what Wu and
Hoskins were
working on....
—Owen

Don't ask me how to handle
this thing. I have no idea
what it is.

If this dinosaur really exists,
I'd say avoid it like the
plague—a plague with razor-sharp
teeth.

—Owen

ADDITIONAL PERSONNEL
Let's get you up to speed with some of the people behind the scenes
of this mission. Everybody's going to be working together on this one.

BENJAMIN LOCKWOOD

Sir Benjamin Lockwood is the philanthropist who's making this mission possible. His foundation will fund a sanctuary for dinosaurs to live in, free from interactions with tourists.

He's in his eighties and in failing health. But his spirit and vision remain strong.

In his youth, he partnered with John Hammond to bring the dinosaurs back to life. The very first dinosaur DNA extraction was made in a lab in Lockwood's subbasement, beneath the mansion where he lives with his granddaughter, Maisie.

Lockwood and Hammond had a falling-out before Hammond died, the nature of which is unknown.

ERUPTION = EXTINCTION

DINOSAURS HAVE RIGHTS TOO

ELI MILLS

Eli Mills has run Lockwood's foundation since he was in college.
He's overseeing the safe removal of dinosaurs from Isla Nublar and their transportation to the sanctuary.
Mills is our contact for all logistical support—transport, medical supplies, weapons, etc.

DINOSAUR
PROTECTION
GROUP

DR. IAN MALCOLM

Dr. Ian Malcolm is a mathematician who specializes in chaos theory.

John Hammond hired him as a consultant, inviting him to Jurassic Park to help evaluate its safety before the park opened.

He is an outspoken critic of cloning dinosaurs and has recently testified before Congress that the dinosaurs should be allowed to die as a result of Isla Nublar's active volcano.

Zia, Let's contact Dr. Malcolm. We've got to change his mind about saving the dinosaurs.

-Claire

DR. HENRY WU

Dr. Henry Wu is the geneticist who has overseen the rebirth of dinosaurs for both Jurassic Park and Jurassic World.

Originally from Ohio, he gained early attention for his undergraduate thesis at MIT. He has a PhD in genetics. InGen hired him in 1986.

Because of his bioethical misconduct, he has been stripped of his credentials. But rumor has it that he is continuing his genetic work for personal gain.

WE WENT TO THE
SAME SCHOOL!?
SO BUMMED ...
—FRANKLIN

PROTECTIVE GEAR AND TRANSPORT

A special mission like ours requires special protective gear.

People. Wear your clawproof vests AT. ALL. TIMES. They could be the reason you come home safe at the end of this mission.

Tranquilizer guns are crucial for sedating the dinosaurs. Some species will require more than one dart to bring them down. Zia is our expert on sedation doses.

—Owen

A little goes a long way.
—Zia

To catch the dinosaurs, we'll need to travel in special military-grade vehicles. These will be heavily armored to help protect against attack. But this is *no guarantee* against destruction by these powerful animals. Be prepared to evacuate the vehicles at any time.

CONTAINED

STG—21
X—433A
734145

DEFEND
ISLA
NUBLAR
OCCUPANTS

Once we have found the dinosaurs and sedated them, we'll need to place them in reinforced containers created specifically for the transport of dinosaurs to the sanctuary island. There are a variety of these metal containers, designed to fit every dinosaur, from the smallest Compy to the largest *T. rex.*

Please acquaint yourselves with the safety features of these vehicles and containers before we arrive on the island. Once there, you'll be able to inspect them in person.

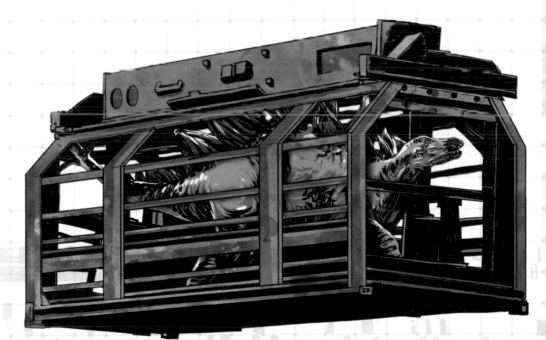

MISSION NOTES

SAVE THE DINOS!